Maddy and Grace at the Haunted House

Gerald Ruhoy

First Edition

PAGE PUBLISHING
Conneaut Lake, PA

First originally published by Page Publishing 2022

ISBN 978-1-6624-6407-2 (hc)
ISBN 978-1-6624-6406-5 (digital)

Printed in the United States of America

Dedicated To:
Madison Hwang

At school, Maddy and Grace kept hearing stories about a haunted house near their neighborhood. None of the kids had ever been in the house, but the scary stories of ghosts, witches, and skeletons were told every day in their classrooms. Maddy asked her mother where the house was and if she thought it was haunted. Her mother told her she didn't believe all those scary stories. She said that when a very old house is empty for a long time, someone is going to say it's haunted. Maddy and Grace were determined to see this house for themselves. This could be an exciting adventure, although a little bit scary.

Grace
MADDY

One Saturday, Maddy and Grace rode their bikes to the part of town where the haunted house was located. This area was very wooded, with some open fields and fences around large properties. Homes were far apart from each other and pretty far off from the main road.

While looking around the area, Maddy and Grace noticed a man fixing fences by the road. They parked their bikes and walked up to him to see if he knew anything about the haunted house. The man said his name was Eric. His job was taking care of many properties, trimming trees, cutting grass, and fixing fences. He said he heard those stories about the haunted house and pointed to where its located, down the road with a "For Sale" sign out front.

RIP
FOR SALE

Maddy and Grace walked to a long dirt driveway that had the "For Sale" sign. The house was not visible from the road because of all the trees and bushes. They went down the dirt driveway to a spot where they could see the house. From a distance, Maddy and Grace saw an old wooden and stone house, very tall and very dark in color. It had many peaks and chimneys. It also had lots of different-shaped windows and ivy covering up to two floors of the house. There was a large shed next to the house where Eric said he keeps his tools and farm equipment when working on the property. From where they stood, Maddy and Grace thought the house looked kind of creepy, and wished they could get a closer look.

Eric told Maddy and Grace that the house had been for sale for a long time. The owners keep lowering the price, but nobody wants to buy it. He said that when people come to look at the house, they stay for only a few minutes and leave in a hurry, very nervous. He told them he saw a real estate agent with her clients coming from the house and actually running to their car to get away as fast as possible. There seems to be something strange going on in this house. Eric said he only takes care of the property and would never go inside. Maybe it is haunted, who knows?
FOR SALE

Maddy and Grace listened to every word Eric was saying. They both felt very creepy just looking at the house from far off. It was getting late, so they decided to head back home. When they got to their bikes, Maddy looked up and saw a couple of bats flying over their heads. All of a sudden, hundreds of bats flew past them in the direction of the haunted house. Maddy and Grace could hardly breathe. They quickly got on their bikes and raced to get out of there. They could hear the loud squeaking sounds of the bats as they frantically pedaled to get home.

MADDY
HAUNTED
OR
NOT?

The next school day, Maddy and Grace told their friends about their trip to the haunted house. They talked about meeting Eric, the story of people running out of the house, and all those bats scaring them as they flew toward the haunted house. Maddy and Grace said they wanted to go back and take close up pictures of the house. Two of their friends said they wanted to go with them. Their names were Jimmy and Bely. Maddy said this was a good idea because there was safety in numbers.

Maddy, Grace, Jimmy, and Bely planned their trip back to the haunted house.

RIP
FOR SALE

The following Saturday, with her phone camera in hand, Maddy, Grace, Jimmy, and Bely headed to the haunted house. When they got to the driveway by the "For Sale" sign, Grace pointed in the direction to where the house was. She told Jimmy and Bely that's where the stories of ghosts, skeletons, giant spiders—

Before she could finish, Jimmy yelled out, "Giant spiders, are you kidding? I'm not going near the place if there are giant spiders!" Maddy told Jimmy he was such a scaredy-cat. She said he could stay there, but we're going closer to get some good pictures. Jimmy sat on a large rock near the "For Sale" sign as Maddy, Grace, and Bely headed down the dirt driveway toward the haunted house. As they approached the house, Maddy kept looking up to see if there were any bats flying around.

As they got closer, the haunted house looked larger and larger, and more creepy looking. Ivy was growing over the first two floors. Some of the windows were cracked, and torn curtains were behind many of them. Shutters were missing or broken. This house was a mess and needed lots of fixing and painting. Maddy took many pictures, then walked up the steps to the front door. The front door was much larger than a normal-size door. It looked very heavy with a crooked iron door handle. Grace and Bely yelled to Maddy to be careful. Everybody was getting nervous. Maddy pushed down on the iron handle and was shocked that the door started to slowly open.

Maddy called Grace and Bely to follow her inside. Everyone was nervous as they walked in. Once inside, they saw a great hall that was dark and dingy. Two wide staircases led up to the second floor. The ceiling was very high, and all the walls were heavy with wood carvings. There were many large doors around the great hall that led to other rooms. As they walked closer to the staircase, they all heard a strange clicking sound coming from the top of the stairs.

Maddy, Grace, and Bely all froze. Their hearts were beating faster. All were staring at the top railing, as the clicking sound kept getting louder. Now they were all shaking as the horrible sound echoed all around them.

MADDY

On the top of the stairs, an ugly skeleton head came up from behind the staircase and spotted Maddy, Grace, and Bely. They all started to scream. The skeleton moved along the railing, making a high-pitched screeching sound. Panicking, Maddy ran to the front door with Grace and Bely right behind her. Maddy grabbed the handle but could not open the door. They were all yelling and screaming. Grace tried the door. It still would not open. Maddy yelled, “It’s locked.” They all ran to the first side door in the hall. It opened, and they quickly ran into the room, slamming the door behind them. They could hear clacking noises coming from the hall. Bely started to cry.

MADDY

The room they were in was a large living area. There were lots of windows but no outside door to escape. They were trapped. From the side of the room, a dark wooden closet door swung open. The girls looked over and saw a tall white thing moving in the closet. It was swaying and making banging sounds against the closet walls. Maddy, screaming, ran to the nearest window. She pushed up as hard as she could but could not open it. Grace and Bely ran over to help. All three pushed on the window. It finally opened. They all were screaming "Ghost" while the banging got louder.

MADDY

Maddy jumped out of the window first. Grace and Bely got stuck trying to get out at the same time. Both were screaming for Maddy to help. By the sound of the banging behind them, it seemed the ghost was getting closer. As Maddy pulled out Grace and Bely, Bely tore her pants on a nail sticking out of the old windowsill. All of them ran like crazy away from the house, tripping and falling on the way. They finally got to Jimmy, exhausted, frightened, and trying to breathe. Maddy told Jimmy that the house was really haunted with a living skeleton and a scary ghost. Jimmy told them to try to calm down because he also saw something very weird.

As everyone was trying to calm down, Jimmy told his story. He said he saw them going into the house which made him nervous. After a few minutes, Jimmy saw this man coming out of the shed, heading up to the front door. He did something, then ran back to the shed. When the girls were screaming and running from the house, Jimmy saw the man coming out of the shed again and running in the opposite direction across the field. When Maddy heard this, she said it had to be Eric. "Why didn't he help us? He had to know we were in trouble. I think he made sure we were trapped. Something is wrong here," Maddy said she is going over to the shed to see if Eric was there. Maddy, Grace, Jimmy, and Bely headed to the shed.

When they got to the shed, they saw two large doors with a lock on them. Maddy went around the side and noticed there was a small window. She called the others over to look. Maddy looked through the window and let out a gulp. There were no tools or farm equipment. There was a large table with three computer screens on top. On the screens were a picture of the great hall as well as other rooms in the house. There also were wires all over the place. Maddy, Grace, Jimmy, and Bely changed from being scared to being mad. Now they could figure out what was going on.

Maddy realized that when Jimmy saw Eric go up to the front door, he was locking it, which trapped them all in the house. He had to be responsible for moving the skeleton and ghost and making all the loud sounds. With all those wires he probably was using some kind of remote control. Then he ran away after hearing us screaming and escaping out the window.

Maddy kept asking why he would do this. They all decided to leave before Eric got back. Maddy said they will call the police when they got home. As they were leaving, everyone was looking around to see if Erik was in the area. They saw no one and quickly got out of there.

MADDY
Grace

Maddy called the police and told them the whole story. The police told Maddy that they would look into it, but she and her friends should never have gone into the house. It's private property. Maddy agreed and said they will never do that again. Grace was at Maddy's house when a policeman came by to talk to them. He said that Eric set up the house to scare people who wanted to buy it. He wanted the sale price to go so low that he would buy it himself and make a huge profit. The policeman thanked Maddy and Grace for ending all the scary stories. He again told them to stay off private property. Maddy and Grace said they learned their lesson.

Everyone at school congratulated Maddy, Grace, Jimmy, and Bely. They were heroes. All the kids asked them a million questions about the haunted house. Maddy told everyone what her mother once told her. Extraordinary claims require extraordinary proof. Maddy felt they met that challenge. Four weeks later, the house was sold to a very nice family. They started fixing it up, cutting down most of the ivy, painting, and repairing the old rotten wood. They also hired a local handyman to help them with their projects. His name was Eric.

CPSIA information can be obtained
at www.ICGtesting.com
Printed in the USA
LVHW071237281222
735360LV00009B/174